W9-CFQ-186

SIDE BY SIDE

ANIMALS WHO HELP EACH OTHER

written by
Marilyn Baillie

illustrated by
Romi Caron

Owl Books

Owl Books are published by Greey de Pencier Books Inc.,
179 John Street, Suite 500, Toronto, Ontario M5T 3G5

OWL and the Owl colophon are trademarks of Owl Communications.
Greey de Pencier Books Inc. is a licensed user of trademarks of Owl Communications.

Distributed in the United States by Firefly Books (U.S.) Inc.,
230 Fifth Avenue, Suite 1607, New York, NY 10001.

This book was published with the generous support of the Canada Council,
the Ontario Arts Council and the Ontario Publishing Centre.

Consultant
Dr. Katherine E. Wynne-Edwards, PhD, Biology Dept., Queen's University, Kingston, Ontario

Dedication
For Charlie, with love.

Author Acknowledgements
A special thank-you to Dr. Katherine Wynne-Edwards for her expertise and generous assistance.
A big thank-you to Publishing Director Sheba Meland and Editor Kat Mototsune for their energy and enthusiasm,
to Julia Naimska for her creative design and to Romi Caron for her engaging illustrations.

Cataloguing in Publication Data
Baillie, Marilyn
Side by side : animals who help each other

(Amazing things animals do)
ISBN 1-895688-56-6 (bound) ISBN 1-895688-57-4 (pbk.)

1. Symbiosis – Juvenile literature. 2. Animal
behavior – Juvenile literature. I. Caron, Romi.
II. Title. III. Series: Baillie, Marilyn. Amazing
things animals do.

QL756.8.B35 1997 j591.52'482 C95-932571-9

Design & Art Direction: Julia Naimska

Photo credits: p. 6, Tui de Roy/Animals Animals;
pp. 8, 28, Luiz C. Marigo/Peter Arnold, Inc.; pp. 10, 16, Norbert Wu/Peter Arnold, Inc.;
p. 12, M. & C. Photography/Peter Arnold, Inc.; p. 14, Stephen J. Krasemann/DRK Photo;
p. 18, Fred Bavendam/Valan Photos; p. 20, Margot Conte/Animals Animals; p. 22, John Cancalosi/Peter Arnold, Inc.;
p. 24, Fritz Pölking/Peter Arnold, Inc.; p. 26, Bill Wood/Bruce Coleman Inc.; pp. 30 – 31, as above.

Printed in Hong Kong

A B C D E F

Contents

HELPING OUT

You live with your family, but there are other very important people in your life, too. Friends and neighbors, teachers and other kids — you help them and they help you. Some animals live side by side with other kinds of animals. They help each other out in surprising ways. Animals can help each other find food or a place to live, or even keep each other safe and healthy. When different animals help each other out, life is a little easier for them.

Animals like the honeyguide bird and the ratel become partners to find and open a beehive. Sometimes many kinds of animals live in the same place and share the food that grows there. This is how giraffes, gerenuks, zebras and gazelles all live together on the African plains.

There are even animals who share their homes. You might find all kinds of animals in the tunnels that prairie dogs dig. How many prairie dogs can you count in this picture? Can you spot another animal who has hopped into a prairie dog burrow to hide? (Answers on page 32.) Now turn the page to meet many amazing animals who live side by side.

Big and Little

How does a giant Galapagos tortoise get rid of the tiny bugs that latch onto her body? Her broad feet are good for holding up her bathtub-sized shell, but they are too clumsy to scratch at the insects. The jagged edge of her mouth is perfect for tearing up food, but no good for nibbling the annoying ticks that bite her leathery skin. She needs help!

To her rescue come hungry finches. The little birds jump around in front of the tortoise to get her attention. The tortoise tilts her shell up, and stretches her neck out as if to say, "Come aboard." The finches hop onto the tortoise and pick the insects off her skin with their tiny beaks. The ticks make a delicious dinner for them. Finally, when they've eaten all the insects, the birds lift their wings and fly away.

MONKEY BUSINESS

Chattering fills the Amazon rain forest, coming closer and closer, getting louder and louder. Branches crack and leaves rustle. Suddenly, there are monkeys everywhere. They swing from branch to branch. They crash through the trees searching for food. The capuchin monkeys lead the way. Up among the higher branches, they grab for fruit and small lizards, and crack open seed pods to eat.

Smaller squirrel monkeys follow along behind. Hungrily they search the leaves for leftovers the capuchins drop. They find and eat insects that have been shaken out of their hiding places. And the more monkeys there are travelling together, the more eyes there are to watch for danger. If one monkey spots the shadow of an eagle, it gives a sharp cry of warning. Suddenly, all the monkeys will hide, leaving the rain forest still and quiet. But soon it will be safe again, and the monkeys will go on their noisy way.

Catch a Ride

A shark glides through the ocean. He will attack and eat almost anything. But does he know a special kind of fish is attached to his body? Fish called remoras stick to the shark using the strong suckers on top of their heads. They ride along, waiting for the shark to find something to eat. The shark eats by tearing at his food with his teeth, and the remoras let go to eat the floating scraps he misses.

When the shark is ready to travel again, the remoras grasp on. They cling to the shark's body, eating the small creatures that live on his skin. The remoras move their suckers along the shark's skin, scraping tiny mites into their open mouths. The remoras keep the shark clean and healthy. In return, the remoras get all the mites and fish scraps they need to eat, and a free ride through the sea.

PROTECTOR ANTS

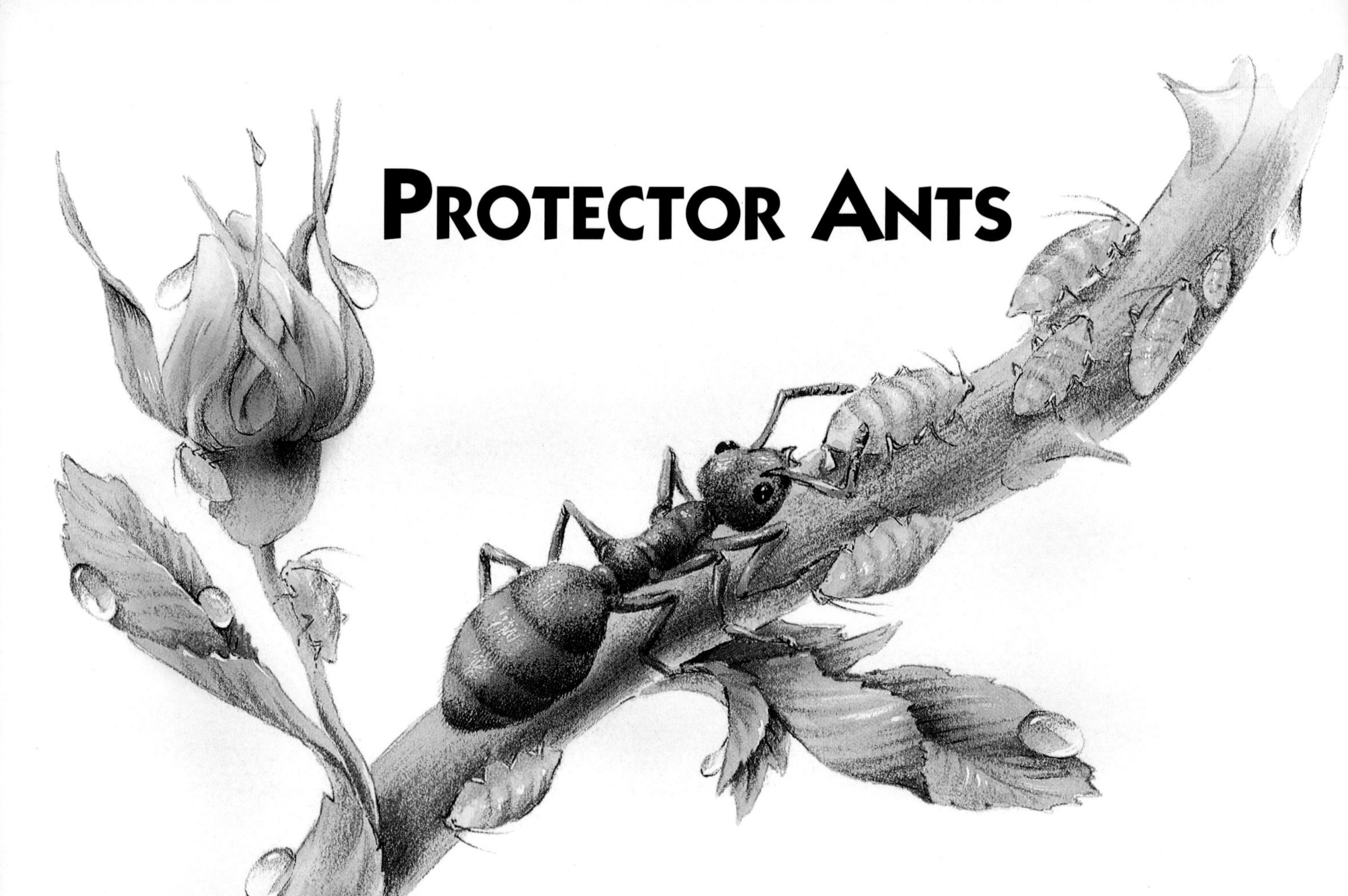

Ants love sweet treats — and they especially love one sweet liquid called honeydew. Tiny green garden insects called aphids make it in their bodies from the plant juices they drink. Ants "milk" honeydew from the aphids almost like a farmer gets milk from a cow. Using its antennae, an ant gently strokes the back of an aphid. Out oozes a drop of delicious honeydew for the ant to sip.

Sometimes ants keep herds of aphids. The ants protect the aphids and care for them. Some ants carry their aphids, one by one, to places where there are good plants to eat. Other ants make tiny mud shelters to protect their aphids from the weather. And some keep their aphids safe in the ant nest at night. Ants that store aphid eggs over the winter are sure to have a new batch of aphids to milk in the spring. And if a hungry ladybug comes looking for aphids to eat, the ants attack it and chase it away.

Rhino Alarm

A rhinoceros and her calf wander from bush to bush, nibbling on branch tips. The huge mother seems calm, but most animals keep their distance from her. Rhinos have sudden tempers, and can attack in an instant. With a swift turn, this mother rhino will charge anything she thinks might threaten her baby. But she doesn't seem to mind the egrets hopping and bobbing at her feet.

As the rhinos walk through the grass, their lumbering feet stir up insects. A surprised grasshopper pops up into the air. Snatch! A waiting egret snaps it up. The egret can find all kinds of insects to eat, including the ticks that live on the rhino's rubbery skin. The egret's sharp eyes also help the rhino mother protect her baby. The egret can spot danger — a hungry hyena — long before the short-sighted rhino mother sees it. The egret flaps its wings, alerting the rhino to keep her baby safe at her side.

Hanging Around

A sloth hangs upside down in a tree. Silent and still, she is hard to spot in the dappled shadows of the rain forest. She moves in slow motion along the branch, drowsily reaching for a leaf to taste. Her baby dozes, cradled by its mother's tummy. Sloths almost never leave the high branches at the tops of the trees. They slowly climb down only to leave their droppings in the ground.

Sloths are so slow, they can be a shelter for smaller animals. Each hair in the sloth's fur is covered with very small scales. Tiny, plantlike creatures called algae live under these scales. The algae make the sloth's fur a greenish color, blending the sloth and her baby into the leafy treetops. Not even a sharp-eyed eagle or hungry jaguar can see them dangling there.

Tiny moths also make their home in the sloth's shaggy coat. Female moths lay eggs in the sloth's droppings. There the eggs become caterpillars and finally change to adult moths. Up into the trees the moths fly, to find homes in the fur of other sloths. Meanwhile, not noticing the algae and moths living on them, the sloth and her baby sleep the day away. Zzzzz.

FISHY FRIENDS

The sea anemone waves its stinging tentacles in the warm tropical sea. Fish that brush against the tips of the bright arms are stunned by the poison there, and are pulled into the anemone's mouth to be eaten. But two clown fish safely dart in and out, around the anemone. They eat the floating bits left over from the anemone's meal. They even live among the poisonous tentacles.

Why are the clown fish not harmed? When they were young, these clown fish chose this sea anemone to live with. The clown fish brushed lightly against the tentacles. Then they quickly pulled away. They rubbed against the stingers again and again, gradually getting used to the poison. In time, they were able to dive into the tentacles and live there. Safe from other fish that might eat them, the clown fish help the anemone, too. Their bright colors attract larger fish looking for a meal. Before they can eat the clown fish, the anemone stings the hunters. They become a meal that the anemone shares with the clown fish.

UNDERGROUND TOWN

The prairie might look deserted from above, but there's a whole town under the ground — a prairie dog town. Hundreds of prairie dogs dig deep into the prairie soil, making dens to live in and tunnels to connect them. They dig lots of burrows — more than they need to live in. So other animals live there too. Snakes sleep through the winter in some dens. Small animals — mice or rabbits — sometimes dart into a tunnel to escape a hunting coyote. Prairie dogs don't seem to mind having neighbors.

Even birds live here. A burrowing owl laid her eggs in an empty prairie dog hole to keep them safe. Her mate keeps watch above ground. The owls could dig their own burrow if they had to. But they found a ready-made tunnel, with the grass around the entrance clipped short by hungry prairie dogs. In the short grass, it's easier for the owl to hunt for grasshoppers and mice. It's easier for him to spot danger at a distance.

At the first sign of danger — a hawk's shadow or the sight of a ferret — a prairie dog will bark, "chirk, chirk!" Then it will shriek a sharp alarm. Others will repeat the warning whistle. In a flash, the owl and prairie dogs will dive into safe burrows. Then all there will be to see above the ground is the golden grass waving in the soft prairie breeze.

ROOMMATES

The petrel spends months fishing for food away from her home. But finally, she returns to her nest in the side of a cliff. Now she will rest and lay her eggs. But what's this? Two eyes shine from inside her hole in the cliff wall. A tuatara has moved in while she was gone. The petrel doesn't chase away the intruder, but settles into her nest with the tuatara as a roommate.

It might seem awfully crowded, but the roommates don't spend a lot of time under the same roof. The tuatara hunts at night and the petrel fishes during the day. The tuatara eats all the bothersome insects in the petrel's nest. It might eat eggs and baby birds from other nests, but not from the nest it shares with the petrel. When the petrel flies out to fish, the tuatara stays behind and keeps the house clean.

GRASSLAND NEIGHBORS

The wide African plain spreads as far as the eye can see. Acacia trees reach up from the vast stretches of grass. You might not think the leaves and grasses found on the plain would provide enough food for many animals to eat. But thousands of animals all graze here — giraffes and gerenuks, zebras and gazelles. They share the food by eating different parts of the plants.

Up, up, the giraffe stretches her neck. Her tough upper lip and long tongue curl around twigs and leaves at the very top of the acacia tree. No other animal can reach so high. At another tree, gerenuks nibble on lower branches. The branches are still too high for most animals to reach. But the gerenuks can balance on their hind legs to get at the leaves and shoots.

Grazing animals share the grasses of the open plains — zebras and Thomson's gazelles all together. The zebras eat the tender tops of the taller grasses. The gazelles get enough food in the shorter, coarser grasses left behind. And if any animal spots a hunting lioness, it gives an alarm that starts hundreds of them all running for safety.

SHINY CLEAN

All kinds of fish live in the coral reef. They swim around, making the ocean bright with flashes of fins and tails. But some fish aren't going anywhere. What are they waiting for? This is a cleaning station in the ocean, like a car wash for your car. Tiny cleaner wrasse fish are on the job. A rainbow of little butterflyfish all wait their turn to be cleaned one by one.

One large angelfish finally has his turn. A little wrasse swims up and down in front of him. Normally, an angelfish would gobble up a small fish so close to his mouth. Is the wrasse letting him know she is part of the clean-up team, and not dinner? The angelfish opens his gill covers and mouth to let the cleaner fish in to nibble. She eats the fungus, dead skin and fish lice he can't reach on his body. Sparkling clean, he swims away. He would never eat the wrasses. They keep him spotless and healthy.

Treat for Two

The honeyguide calls as she flies, dipping and swooping. Her tail fans out, showing off the white feathers. On the ground, a furry companion follows along. The ratel growls softly, as together they head for a honeybee nest. The honeyguide loves to eat beeswax and the grubs that will grow up into bees. The ratel eats insects, plants, small animals and fruit — but honey is a special treat.

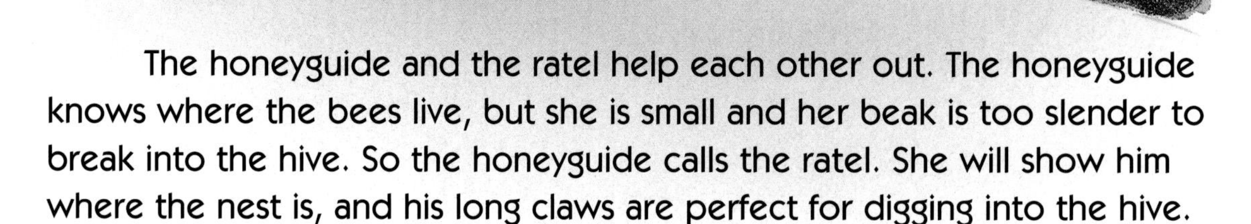

The honeyguide and the ratel help each other out. The honeyguide knows where the bees live, but she is small and her beak is too slender to break into the hive. So the honeyguide calls the ratel. She will show him where the nest is, and his long claws are perfect for digging into the hive.

The bird's song changes as she leads the ratel to where the nest is hidden in a hollow tree. He rubs the smelly scent from under his tail all over the nest opening. The smell stuns the bees so they cannot sting. Then the ratel can rip into the nest, and the honeyguide joins in. Mmmm, sweet honey and delicious bee grubs!

WHO'S WHO

GIANT TORTOISE AND DARWIN'S GROUND FINCH

The giant tortoise and Darwin's ground finch live on the Galapagos Islands. The tortoise can grow during its whole long life to reach the size of a bathtub. The ground finch is about the size of your fist. It was named for Charles Darwin, who studied many animals found only on the Galapagos.

ANTS AND APHIDS

Ants live almost everywhere in the world except cold polar areas. In their groups, called colonies, work is shared and each ant has a special job. Aphids are green and about the size of the lead poking out of a pencil. Because they suck juices out of plants, they are pests in gardens.

SQUIRREL MONKEY

Capuchin monkeys and squirrel monkeys live in South American forests. Squirrel monkeys are like squirrels in their size and because they use their long tails for balance as they climb and jump. Capuchins are about the size of large cats, and usually stay high in the tops of the rain forest trees.

RHINOCEROS AND CATTLE EGRETS

Rhinoceroses are found in dry bush and scrub areas in Africa. An adult rhino is about the size of a small car. Cattle egrets are originally from Africa, but have spread to North and South America and even Australia. A cattle egret would be a little taller than the seat of a chair.

BLUE SHARK

Sharks come in many shapes and sizes. But all have many rows of sharp teeth they use to tear at the food they find in the coastal seas where they swim. Remoras are fish that live in tropical and temperate seas. A remora can be as long as your hand or even longer than your arm.

THREE-TOED SLOTH

The three-toed sloth lives in the rain forests of Central and South America. Its body is about the size of a big cat, but its arms are very long so it can hang from trees. More than a hundred sloth moths might live on one sloth. Each dull brown moth is about the length of your thumbnail.

Clown Fish and Sea Anemone

Clown fish swim in warm, shallow ocean waters, especially the Red Sea and the Indo-Pacific Ocean. A clown fish is about the size of your hand held flat. Sea anemones come in many sizes and bright colors. They can be as small as a toothbrush or as big as a bush, and their tentacles can be long and feathery or short and stubby.

Giraffe and Zebra

Giraffes, gerenuks, Thomson's gazelles and zebras all live on the plains of East Africa. The giraffe is the tallest animal in the world. Zebras are just like striped horses. The gerenuk is about the size of a goat, and is sometimes called the giraffe-gazelle because of its long neck. The delicate Thomson's gazelles are smaller still.

Black-tailed Prairie Dog

Home for black-tailed prairie dogs is the North American plains. They dig tunnels and burrows to make whole towns underground. A prairie dog is the size of a very small dog. Burrowing owls also live on the North American prairie. They are about the size of robins, and hunt during the day and evening.

Cleaner Wrasse and Grouper

Cleaner wrasse fish set up cleaning stations in corral reefs, alone or in groups of two or three. A wrasse is about the length of a grown-up's finger. Butterflyfish and angelfish live in tropical waters in the Indo-Pacific. Butterflyfish are only about as long as your hand, but angelfish can be as long as a grown-up's arm.

Tuatara

Tuataras are lizard-like reptiles that live only on the islands off the coast of New Zealand. A tuatara is only about as long as your arm, but it is related to dinosaurs. Diving petrels are about the size of seagulls, and they fish the seas of the southern hemisphere. They gather in large groups to nest in holes in the rocks of cliffs overlooking the sea.

Ratel

Ratels are a little bigger than skunks, with the same black and white fur and long claws for digging. Also called honey badgers, they live in Africa, Asia and India. The honeyguide bird lives near forests in East and Central Africa. It is small enough to fit on the palm of your hand. People, as well as ratels, follow the honeyguide to find honey.

Who Am I?

Here's a quiz for you to try. Each clue tells you how two animals live side by side. Which animal is speaking? And can you name its animal friend, too?

1. When I'm out fishing, I leave a roommate in my nest who helps keep it clean.
2. I glide through the sea, attached to another by a sucker on top of my head.
3. We live together in Africa, where the trees and grasses feed us all.
4. My touch is poisonous to most fish, but not to the ones that live in my tentacles.
5. Colorful fish wait patiently for me to clean them at my underwater station.
6. In the Galapagos, I eat insects that live on the skin and large shell of my friend.
7. We crash through the rain forest in noisy groups, and I eat the insects that are disturbed when others break branches and eat fruit high in the treetops.
8. I hang in the branches high off the ground, and let little insects live in my long fur.
9. I lead my partner to a bee nest and he tears it open so we can eat the honey, wax and bee grubs.
10. I give my keepers sweet food, and they take care of us in herds.
11. Birds eat insects that jump from my path, and warn me of danger to my baby.
12. We dig lots of tunnels and burrows underground, and others build their nests and hatch their eggs in our town, too.

Answers

Helping Out, p. 5: There are 31 prairie dogs; a rabbit has hopped into an empty burrow.

Who Am I? p. 32: 1. Diving Petrel, Tuatara; 2. Remora, Shark; 3. Giraffe, Gerenuk, Thomson's Gazelle, Zebra; 4. Sea Anemone, Clown fish; 5. Cleaner Wrasse, Butterflyfish and Angelfish; 6. Ground Finch, Giant Tortoise; 7. Squirrel Monkey, Capuchin Monkey; 8. Three-toed Sloth, Sloth Moth; 9. Honeyguide, Ratel; 10. Aphid, Ants; 11. Rhinoceros, Cattle Egret; 12. Black-tailed Prairie Dog, Burrowing Owl.